HOWL-A-WEEN

TODD
STRASSER

D1368038

AN
APPLE
PAPERBACK

SCHOLASTIC INC.
New York Toronto London Auckland Sydney

To Emily, Alex, and Willy Seife

If you purchased this book without a cover, you should be aware that this book is stolen property. It was reported as "unsold and destroyed" to the publisher, and neither the author nor the publisher has received any payment for this "stripped book."

No part of this publication may be reproduced in whole or in part, or stored in a retrieval system, or transmitted in any form or by any means, electronic, mechanical, photocopying, recording, or otherwise, without written permission of the publisher. For information regarding permission, write to Scholastic Inc., 555 Broadway, New York, NY 10012.

ISBN 0-590-64933-7

Copyright © 1995 by Todd Strasser. All rights reserved. Published by Scholastic Inc. APPLE PAPERBACKS and the APPLE PAPERBACKS logo are registered trademarks of Scholastic Inc.

12 11 10 9 8 7 6 5 4 3 2 1   5 6 7 8 9/9 0/0

Printed in the U.S.A.   40

First Scholastic printing, October 1995

1

"Okay, so listen to this one," Scott said. "Moe, Larry, and Curly find this magic lamp."

"Where?" asked Emily.

"It doesn't matter where," said Scott. "They just find this lamp and they rub it."

"They *all* rub it?" asked Emily.

"No, they don't *all* rub it," Scott replied. "One of them rubs it."

"Which one?" asked Emily.

"It doesn't *matter* which one!" Scott was getting flustered. He always gets flustered when things don't go his way.

"It does to me," said Emily, who likes to be exact.

Scott and Emily are my two closest friends. Scott is a shrimp with straight blond hair and a big nose. Emily is a tall, gawky girl with curly red hair and freckles. Scott is the smallest boy in the eighth grade. Emily is the tallest person in the eighth grade. They'd make quite a pair if it wasn't for me. My name is Kate. I have purple hair with orange and yellow streaks, a nose ring, and a pierced belly button.

Just kidding . . .

Actually my hair is mouse-brown. My problem is I'm boring. It's not really my fault. I get it from my parents. It's one of those genetic things. Our last name is Smith. There are probably some exciting Smiths out there somewhere, but not us. We're the genetically boring Smiths.

"Emily, it's just a joke," I reminded her. "Go ahead, Scott."

"Thanks, Kate," Scott said. "Anyway, one of them rubs the lamp and out pops this genie."

Emily raised her hand.

"Now what?" Scott groaned.

"Am I allowed to ask one tiny teensy itsy bitsy little question?" asked Emily.

Scott let out an exaggerated sigh. "Go ahead."

"Was it, like, a normal genie or a big blue Robin-Williams-type genie?"

"Normal."

"Good, thanks."

In case you're wondering, Emily, Scott, and I were walking down King Street toward Paloma Federici's farm stand. Well, actually, it's Paloma's grandfather's farm stand. But every year Paloma has a Halloween pumpkin-carving party and she invites her friends.

Paloma insists that we go to the party in our Halloween costumes. She's been having her pumpkin-carving party since we were five years old. Last year, in seventh grade, kids began to grumble about wearing costumes. After all, we were seventh-graders, and too cool to get dressed up like vampires and ghosts. But Paloma insisted, so we did.

This year a lot of kids actually decided not to go to the party if it meant dressing up. Scott didn't want to go, and Emily wasn't too keen about it either. But I begged them to do it one last time. It had been a very boring fall and I wanted to have some fun.

Anyway, back to Scott's joke.

"So this genie pops out of the lamp," Scott went on.

Emily sheepishly raised her hand.

"For Pete's sake!" Scott cried. "*Now* what?"

"I'm sorry," Emily said. "I just have to know why."

"Why what?"

"Why a genie came out of the lamp."

"Because genies *always* come out of lamps, that's why!" Scott yelled.

"That's not true," replied Emily.

Scott's eyes started to bug out. I decided to intervene before he went ballistic. "Excuse me, Emily. I'd just like to remind you that Scott did

3

state before that it was a *magic* lamp. Therefore I think it's safe to assume that if you rub it a genie will pop out."

"Thank you, Kate." Scott started to calm down. "May I continue, Emily?"

Emily shrugged. "I guess."

"So the genie pops out and says he'll grant them three wishes," Scott said. "And in case you're wondering, Emily, I don't know why it was *three* wishes and not seven wishes, or even ten thousand wishes. Actually, I don't even know *why* he granted them any wishes at all. He just did, okay?"

Emily nodded and didn't say a thing.

"Good," Scott said. "Now where was I?"

Before I could remind him, we heard the scraping sound of urethane wheels on the pavement behind us. Turning around, we saw a dozen skater dudes weaving down the street. They were wearing baggy pants, sweatshirts, and baseball caps backwards on their heads.

Emily, Scott, and I shared a wary glance.

We had a problem.

And this was no joke.

2

The leader of the skater dudes was a kid named Lewis Larson. Lewis is a tall, skinny guy with a brown buzz-cut, lots of gold hoops in his ears, and a very active zit farm on his face. He is what some of us in the eighth grade at Bernardsville Middle School call a major scuzzball.

Lewis skidded his board to a stop near us, then stepped on the back, making it flip up into his hands.

"Whoa!" He pointed at us with a mean smirk. "Check out the geeks."

The painful truth was that this was not the first time Emily, Scott, and I had heard ourselves called geeks. If you are a small boy with a big nose, or a big, gawky girl with freckles, or a genetically boring person, it is possible that you too have been called this name.

Of course, being dressed in Halloween costumes didn't help.

"And who are you supposed to be?" Lewis asked

Scott. The other skater dudes snickered. Scott was wearing green pants with suspenders, a red plaid shirt, and a green felt hat that was too large for his head. He was carrying a long stick that ended in a curve — like an oversize cane.

Scott turned and glared at me. At that moment he really hated me because I was the one who'd convinced him to wear a costume.

"I'm waiting, shrimp," Lewis Larson said.

"The Boy Who Cried Wolf," Scott mumbled unhappily.

"Aw, isn't that cute?" Lewis and the skater dudes guffawed. Then he turned to me. "And what about you?"

To avoid needless duplication, Paloma always assigned costume themes a week before her party. Scott, Emily, and I had the misfortune of being assigned *Famous Fairy Tale Liars*.

"You can't be that thick, Lewis," I replied. After all, I was wearing lederhosen, a felt hat, white gloves, and a fake ten-inch wooden nose.

Lewis's pimply face hardened.

"Come on, man," said one of the skater dudes behind him. "Don't you know it's — "

"Shuddup!" Lewis snapped at him. Then he glowered at me. I wasn't certain whether he was trying to figure out who I was supposed to be, or how he was going to kill me.

"Uh, like, one of the seven dwarves?" he finally guessed.

6

The other skater dudes groaned in disbelief.

"Yo dummy, she's Pinocchio," yelled one of them.

"No way," Lewis protested. "She's a chick."

"No law says a chick can't be Pinocchio," another skater dude said.

"And besides, the seven dwarves were all guys," added a third.

"They were?" Lewis scratched his head and frowned.

The other skater dudes gave each other looks, as if they couldn't believe how dumb Lewis was.

Meanwhile, Lewis turned to Emily. He had to look up, since Emily was taller than he. "And who are *you* supposed to be?"

I'm sure that in some middle school somewhere is a girl of Emily's height and size who would have reared back and slugged Lewis straight up to the big half-pipe in the sky. But this particular Emily is too shy and reserved ever to do such a thing.

"Look, Lewis, this really isn't fair." I came to her rescue. "We were assigned a really hard category. There weren't a lot of choices."

"I just asked who she was supposed to be," Lewis growled.

Emily muttered something under her breath.

"Huh? I didn't hear you."

Again Emily muttered something we couldn't hear. I guess I should mention that over her nose and mouth she was wearing an orange cardboard mask that resembled a bird's beak. The rest of her was encased in a large garbage bag covered with white feathers from an old down pillow. We'd sprayed the bag with adhesive and then sprinkled the feathers on it.

"I still didn't hear you," Lewis grumbled.

"Chicken Little." It was barely a whisper, but loud enough for everyone to hear.

3

The skater dudes started convulsing all over the street. You would have thought this was the funniest thing since *Beavis and Butt-head*. Some were laughing so hard that they were doubled over and holding their stomachs. Others were wiping tears out of their eyes.

"Did you hear that!?"

"Chicken *Little*!?"

"Turkey Lurkey's more like it!"

Emily stood stiffly with her face drawn into a tight, mute expression. None of this was the least bit fair or true. Emily is actually extremely pretty and maybe even beautiful. It was just that she'd grown bigger and faster than the rest of us. Certain people, mostly boys, seemed to have a hard time dealing with that.

"Don't listen to them," whispered Scott.

"Let's just go," I said.

Since Lewis and the other skater dudes were still busy yucking it up, we left them and continued toward the party. But about halfway down the block, the sound of scraping skateboard wheels again caught up to us.

"So you're going to that stupid Halloween party." Lewis cut a figure eight with his board in front of us.

"What makes you think that?" I asked.

Lewis scowled. "Because you're wearing those dumb costumes."

"But we always dress like this," I said. You may have noticed that I have a sassy mouth. It's something I've developed to compensate for being genetically boring.

Meanwhile, Lewis scratched his head again. I think he was trying to figure out if what I'd said was true.

"Uh, dude?" One of his friends tapped him on the shoulder.

"What?" Lewis asked.

"I think she's pulling your leg."

Lewis's face turned red and he squinted angrily at us. "Well, I've got news for you nerdwarts. Tonight we're gonna steal every jack-o'-lantern in town. Then we're gonna put 'em in a big pile in the middle of Cedar Street and blow 'em up."

"Right, Lewis." I rolled my eyes in disbelief.

"You don't believe me?" Lewis turned and waved to a kid named Alex. Alex skated toward us on his board. He had brown hair parted in the middle and wore a baggy green Army-surplus jacket that was about eight sizes too big.

"Show 'em," Lewis said.

Alex's eyes darted around nervously as if he was afraid someone might see. "You sure?"

"Yeah." Lewis nodded.

From inside his jacket, Alex took out something about the size of a softball and wrapped in aluminum foil.

"Know what that is?" Lewis asked us.

"Last week's lunch?" I guessed.

"It's a subatomic molecular pumpkin disorganizer," Lewis said. "Alex made it by scraping the black powder out of caps."

"Are you serious?" asked Scott, who takes a boyish interest in such things.

Alex nodded.

"How long did it take you to make it?" Scott asked.

"Two years," Alex announced.

"*Two years!?*" I gasped in total disbelief. "You spent two years making *that?*"

"Sure," Alex said. "I had to scrape the powder from seven hundred eighty-six rolls of caps. If you figure there are a hundred caps per roll, that's seventy-eight thousand, six hundred caps."

For a moment there was dead silence as we stared at him in total wonder.

Finally, I cleared my throat. "I don't know if

anyone's ever told you this before, Alex. But you are one sick puppy."

Alex smiled proudly as if I'd just given him a great compliment. Then he slid the aluminum foil subatomic molecular pumpkin disorganizer back into his jacket and skateboarded away.

"So if you want to see something awesome tonight," Lewis said, "come to Cedar Street."

"Wouldn't miss it for the world," I said as sarcastically as I could.

Emily, Scott, and I watched Lewis and his skater friends push off and weave away down the street.

"Do you think Lewis was born that stupid?" Scott asked. "Or was it something he really had to work hard at?"

"Let's forget about him and go to the party," I said. Emily was staring down at the ground with her shoulders stooped. I knew her feelings must've been hurt from the mean things Lewis had said.

"You okay?" I asked.

Emily shrugged silently and we continued toward the farm stand. I felt bad because I was the one who'd insisted we wear these dumb costumes. I guess I just couldn't bear the idea of another boring Halloween.

Little did I know . . .

4

We were on the edge of town, where the houses start to give way to farm fields. The Federicis' farm stand was about a quarter of a mile down the road. We could see that the party had already begun. In the field behind the farm stand, kids dressed as famous fairy tale braggarts, heroes, and villains were hunting around for pumpkins to carve.

"How come the Federicis always give away pumpkins on Halloween Day?" Scott asked as we walked.

"They only give them to the kids who come to the party," I said. "And anyway, the only ones left are the rejects and mutants."

"What's a mutant pumpkin?" Emily asked.

"One that's shaped weird, or soft on one side, or a yucky color."

"The geeks of the vegetable world," Emily said with a weary sigh.

"You sure you don't mean the *leeks* of the vegetable world?" asked Scott, the punster.

"Yuck, yuck," I said, deadpan. "Paloma told me that this year they tried a new genetically engineered fertilizer on their pumpkins. But something was wrong with the formula and they got a lot of mutants in strange shapes and sizes."

"Are you sure they're safe?" Emily asked nervously.

"Well, Paloma did say that a few glowed in the dark. But they got rid of those."

"Too bad," said Scott. "If they glowed by themselves, you wouldn't need candles. It would be like growing a ready-made jack-o'-lantern."

"Wouldn't that sort of take the fun out of it?" Emily asked.

"Hey, guys, wait up!" a voice shouted. We turned and saw a large, round ball of white fuzz lumbering down the street toward us. The fuzz ball was carrying a white paper shopping bag in each hand.

"Who is that?" Emily asked.

"I think you mean, *what* is that?" said Scott.

"Bobby-Lee Boyle," I said. If Scott was one of the smallest boys in the grade, then Bobby-Lee was one of the fattest.

Bobby-Lee slowed to a walk while we waited for him. He was almost unrecognizable inside his ball of white fuzz.

"Let me guess," said Scott. "You're cotton candy?"

"Close," Bobby-Lee replied. "Paloma ran out of fairy tale stuff, so she assigned me medical supplies."

"A cotton ball?" guessed Emily.

"Actually, I started out as a Q-Tip, but I lost my stick," Bobby-Lee said.

"What's in the bags?" I asked.

"Candy," Bobby-Lee announced.

"You've already started trick-or-treating?"

"Better believe it," said Bobby-Lee. "Before the night is over, I plan to trick-or-treat at every house in Bernardsville. Last year I only missed by eleven houses."

"How many bags did you fill?" Emily asked.

"Four-and-a-half."

"Four-and-a-half shopping bags of candy?" Scott asked in amazement. We all started toward Paloma's party. "How long did it take to eat all of it?"

"One year," Bobby-Lee replied. "I divided the candy into fifty-two Ziploc bags and ate one bag a week. You know how much allowance I was able to save because I didn't have to buy candy?"

"How much?" Emily asked.

"Almost two hundred dollars," Bobby-Lee announced proudly.

"And what did you do with that?" I asked.

Bobby-Lee scowled at me as if the answer should have been very obvious. "Bought ice cream, what else?"

Tell me the Bernardsville Middle School doesn't have its share of colorful characters.

5

The first thing we saw at the party was a sign:

CAUTION

DO NOT PICK GLOWING PUMPKINS.

Due to an error in the formulization of a new fertilizer, some pumpkins in this field have been found to glow in the dark. Tests conducted by the state indicate that these pumpkins ARE NOT HARMFUL. However, just to be safe, we urge you not to pick them.

HAPPY HALLOWEEN!
The Federici Family

"Guess we shouldn't pick the glowing pumpkins," Scott said.

"We'll be lucky to find *any* pumpkins," said Bobby-Lee.

He was right. Most of the pumpkins near the

17

farm stand had already been picked by the other kids. Finding even a reject mutant pumpkin was going to be hard. Emily, Scott, Bobby-Lee, and I trudged through the field behind the stand, sorting through the green vines.

"Found one!" Emily reached under a vine and held up something orange and the size of a tennis ball.

"You'll never get a candle inside it," Scott said.

"Maybe one of those little skinny birthday candles," said Bobby-Lee.

"Well, I love it." Emily gently rubbed the dirt off her pumpkin with her fingers. She looked like a big white bird with a little orange egg. "See you guys back at the party."

Emily headed back toward the picnic tables where kids in Halloween costumes sat carving their pumpkins.

Soon Scott and Bobby-Lee also found reject mutant nonglowing pumpkins of their own.

"Come on, Kate," Scott said impatiently. "Let's get back to the party."

"We're gonna miss the food if we don't go soon," urged Bobby-Lee.

"You guys go ahead," I said.

"Why can't you just pick a pumpkin and be done with it?" Scott asked.

"Because these are all mutant rejects."

"But that's all that's left," said Scott. "Besides,

it's getting late. In another half hour, it's gonna be dark."

Scott pointed to the west, where the sun was a large orange orb just a little bit higher than the trees.

"Sorry, I didn't come all this way to pick someone's mutant reject," I said.

"Come on, Kate," said Bobby-Lee. "It's not that important. Just pick one."

"My parents taught me never to settle for anything less than perfection," I said. Actually, that wasn't true. But I had other reasons for seeking the right one.

"We're talking about a stupid pumpkin," Scott said.

"Don't call them stupid," I warned. "You'll hurt their feelings."

Scott rolled his eyes and started back toward the farm stand. "See you at the party . . . *if* you make it."

"Guess I'll go back, too," said Bobby-Lee. "Don't get lost, Kate."

I watched as the Boy Who Cried Wolf and the world's largest cotton ball headed back across the field toward the party. Then I turned and kept looking. I didn't care if it took me all night to find the right pumpkin. I was a Pinocchio with a mission.

6

You're probably wondering why it was so important for me to find the right pumpkin. Basically, it was because of boringness. Not only do I have boring parents, I also have a boring brother, a boring house, even a boring dog. For most of my life I accepted boringness as my fate. But then I became thirteen.

It was time to rebel.

It was time to find a pumpkin that reflected the way I felt.

A pumpkin that was not boring.

I went farther out into the fields than anyone else — past all the other kids' footsteps.

I passed up several serious mutant pumpkin contenders.

Then I noticed a glow coming from under some trees at the very edge of the field. Curious, I went over to take a look. There, under some vines and broad green leaves, was a pumpkin.

I hesitated, recalling the warning about glowing pumpkins.

But this one wasn't really glowing.

Not *that* much.

Besides, the state had tested the glowing pumpkins and determined that they were not harmful.

I'm a big believer in state testing.

7

A few minutes later I staggered up to the picnic tables with my pumpkin. Oddly, it had stopped glowing altogether.

"What is *that*?" asked Scott, looking up from his apple cider and carrot cake. All the other kids had finished carving their jack-o'-lanterns and were also eating.

"A pumpkin," I said simply, laying it down on the picnic table.

"Are you sure?" asked Emily.

"It's orange, isn't it?" I asked.

"Well, yes."

"And I found it in a pumpkin field, right?" I said.

"If you say so."

"Then what's the problem?"

"It's not *shaped* like a pumpkin," Emily said.

She was right. Instead of being round, it was

shaped like a frog's head. There were two big bumps where the eyes would go, and a slanted jutting jaw for the mouth.

And I loved it because it was anything but boring.

8

"I saw the pumpkin you brought home," my mother said at dinner as she scooped mashed potatoes out of a bowl and onto her plate. I had come home after the party to have another boring dinner with my boring family.

"What about it?" I asked innocently as I cut into my meatloaf.

"Did you see it?" my mother asked my father, who was mixing his mashed potatoes with his green peas.

"No," said my father, who is bald and has glasses and always wears a white shirt.

"It's . . . unusual," said my mother, who has short, mouse-brown hair like mine, and wears plain brown dresses and no makeup or jewelry.

"How come?" asked my brother, Ben, as he drank a glass of milk. Ben was wearing a plaid short-sleeved shirt.

"The shape," said my mother.

"Worried about what the neighbors may think?" I asked.

"Well, I guess it's all right for tonight," allowed my mother.

"What's tonight?" asked my father.

"It's Halloween, Dad."

"Oh, right, of course." Dad nodded. Apparently he'd forgotten.

"That's why I'm wearing lederhosen, a felt hat, and a ten-inch stick for a nose," I said.

"I was going to ask you about that," said Dad.

"If you'd like, I'll make a pumpkin pie with it tomorrow," suggested our housekeeper, Doris, as she brought over a bowl of salad made with iceberg lettuce, carrots, and celery.

"I thought maybe we could leave it on the porch until it rots," I said. "I know winter's coming and it's getting cold, so it may not rot until next spring. But I'd like to see it happen. I picked it because I thought it might have a high rotability quotient. Like maybe it'll turn brown and start to settle and smell really bad. Maybe it'll attract ants or mice or something."

My mother gave my father a weary look, as if maybe someone had switched babies on her in the hospital.

"So who are you going trick-or-treating with?" asked Ben.

"Emily and Scott. We're going as famous fairy

tale liars. Scott's the Boy Who Cried Wolf and Emily is Chicken Little."

"I'm not sure I'd call Chicken Little a liar," said my father, who is an engineer and very precise.

"Deluded would be more like it," said my mother, who is a pediatrician and has an office in the house.

"Or just plain dumb," said my brother, Ben, who's in tenth grade and spends most of his time in cyberspace.

"Well, it was a toss up between Chicken Little and Tinkerbell," I said. "Either way it was a no-win situation for Emily."

Fred the dog went *yip*. Fred is a medium-sized shaggy brown mutt who sleeps all day and never wants to play or fetch or do anything fun. Once in a while he'll get up and go over to the kitchen door and go *yip*. That means he wants to go out. I've never even heard him bark.

I let Fred out. It had gotten dark during dinner. The streetlights had come on. In the distance I could hear some *pops!* and *bangs!* as kids set off fireworks.

"Geneva Datelin brought her daughter into the office today," my mother was saying when I went back into the kitchen. "The silly girl had gotten her lip pierced and it got infected."

My father shook his head in wonder. "Why do these kids want to pierce themselves?"

"It gives me the shivers," my mother said. "The thought of these kids with strange pieces of jewelry hanging from various parts of their bodies."

"I guess they think it's cool," I said, sitting down at the kitchen table again.

"I'll tell you what's cool," said Ben. "The new Dalton Systems Algorithmic Spread Sheet program I just got."

Mom and Dad gave each other concerned looks. Except for school, Ben hadn't left the house for weeks.

"Ben, dear, did you see the canoe your father and I got you for your birthday?" Mom asked.

It was hard to miss. My parents had left it in the front hall so we saw it every time we left or returned to the house.

"Yes," said Ben. "What am I supposed to do with it?"

"We thought you might use it on the lake," Mom said. "You really should get outside more."

"But I like being inside," Ben said.

"We know you do, sweetheart," said Mom. "But it isn't good to be inside all the time. Young people should get out once in a while."

"Dad said he never went outside when he was a kid," Ben said. "And he hardly ever goes out these days either, unless it's to work or the lumber yard."

Mom and Dad gave each other a look.

"Ahem." Dad cleared his throat. "Well, to tell you the truth, Ben, I wish I had gone outdoors more as a young man."

"Then why don't you go out more now?" I asked.

Mom and Dad both glowered at me for a moment.

"Your father is very hard at work restoring this house," Mom said.

We live in a big old Victorian house with green trim. It's three stories tall and has a big porch in the front. When my parents bought it ten years ago, it was falling apart. Their major hobby is restoring it. When they're finished, they want it to look exactly like it did in 1894.

Yawn.

"That reminds me," Dad said. "I've got to finish carving the new balusters for the stairs tonight."

"What are balusters?" I asked.

"Those short round poles that hold up the railings for stairs," Dad said. "I'm carving a whole set of them on my lathe."

"Sounds really exciting, Dad," I said sarcastically.

"It just so happens that it takes a great deal of precision to carve a set of twenty identical balusters," Dad said.

I pretended to yawn.

Mom and Dad shared another look. Then Mom turned to me. "I've noticed lately that you seem unhappy with us. Would you prefer a different set of parents?"

"No, I'd just like you guys to change a little," I said.

"How?" asked my father.

"Well, I don't mean to hurt your feelings or anything, but maybe you could just be a little less boring."

Mom and Dad both looked surprised.

Ding-dong! Just then the doorbell rang.

"Who could that be?" asked my father.

"A trick-or-treater, probably," said Ben.

"Oh, dear, I forgot to get candy," said my mother. "Doris, would you go into my office, get the bag of lollipops, and put them in a bowl?"

Doris left and came back with a bag of lollipops. They were the cheap, thin, flat, round kind that came in green, yellow, and red. The boring kind. Doris took a bowl out of the cupboard and poured in the lollipops.

"I'll take it," I said. Bowl in hand, I started out of the kitchen. As I walked down the long hallway to the front door, I passed the stained glass windows with floral designs. I passed the big glass display cases filled with my mother's collection of old china plates and miniature ceramics. I walked under the antique crystal chandelier that hung from the ceiling.

Then I passed the big wooden staircase leading

to the second floor. Ben's new canoe was lying on the floor beside the staircase.

I opened the front door. Outside on the porch were seven little kids all wearing multicolored Power Prince Parakeet costumes. The Power Prince Parakeets were the latest TV rage.

"Here you go," I said, holding out the bowl of lollipops.

The first Power Prince Parakeet looked in the bowl and made a face. "Haven't you got anything better than that?"

"Sorry," I said.

"What is this, a dentist's office?" asked another Power Prince Parakeet.

"The dentist wouldn't give you sweets," I said. "My mother's a pediatrician."

"*Borrrrriiinnnnggg,*" the kid groaned, and took a lollipop.

How quickly they learn.

9

The Power Prince Parakeets went back down the front steps and off into the dark to find houses offering better candy. I was just about to close the front door when I noticed a slight glow coming from the porch. Stepping out I saw that it was coming from my pumpkin.

"Hey, Pinocchio!" someone yelled. Looking up, I spotted the Boy Who Cried Wolf and Chicken Little passing under a streetlight on the corner.

"I'll be right with you guys," I yelled and went back into the house.

Back in the kitchen I opened a drawer and took out some matches for my jack-o'-lantern. Then I grabbed a shopping bag and stopped by the kitchen table where my family was still eating.

"See you later," I said.

"Make sure you're home by nine, sweetheart," said my mother.

"Be careful," said my father.

"If you see any candy apples, bring one home for me, okay?" asked Ben.

"Sure," I said. "And don't do anything too exciting while I'm gone, okay?"

My parents smiled weakly. It was a joke. About the most interesting thing they ever did was rearrange the furniture.

I went out the front door and onto the porch. Our porch spanned the whole front of the house. The roof above it was held up by big white columns. Sometimes on a warm summer night my parents sat on the porch sipping lemonade and watching the cars go by.

Exciting, huh?

"How was dinner?" Emily asked as she and Scott came up the porch steps.

"Boring as usual." I kneeled next to my pumpkin, which was no longer glowing. I took the top off and struck a match. "I just wish, just once, that my family would lose control and act totally crazy."

As I said that, I lit the candle inside the jack-o'-lantern.

10

*F*WOOOOOOOM! The next thing I knew, a huge column of sparkling light and flame burst out of the jack-o'-lantern.

"Ahhhh!" I yelped in surprise and jumped back.

"What was that?" Emily gasped.

But as quickly as it had appeared, the light and flame disappeared, leaving just the flickering light of the candle inside the pumpkin.

"It must have been some kind of flare," Scott said, peering into the pumpkin.

"How'd it get there?" I asked. My heart was pounding from the surprise.

"I bet Lewis and his skater friends did it," Scott said. "Just a Halloween prank."

"How come I don't smell any smoke?" Emily asked. "Usually fireworks have that gunpowder smell."

"Must be some new, odorless kind." Scott

shrugged. "Anyway, let's go. I want to get some candy."

We went down the porch steps, across the driveway, and into the street. It was a dark, moonless night. As we crossed to the other corner, I happened to glance back at my house. I thought I saw something strange and stopped.

"What's wrong?" Scott asked.

"Do you see anything weird about my house?" I asked.

Scott and Emily looked back, then shook their heads. "No, why?"

"I just looked back there a second ago and I could swear the whole house was glowing."

"It's probably just your eyes," Scott said. "From being so close to that flare before."

"I don't think so," I said. "It was different than that."

"Then welcome to the Twilight Zone," Emily said.

11

We went trick-or-treating.

"Let me guess," people would say when they opened their front doors. "You're Pinocchio and you're . . . uh . . ."

"The theme is famous fairy tale liars." I'd give them a hint.

"Oh, so you must be the Boy Who Cried Wolf," they'd say to Scott. Then they'd turn to Emily. "And you're, uh, hmmm . . ."

Most people had a hard time guessing that Emily was Chicken Little.

"Maybe I should have Chicken Little tattooed across my forehead," Emily moped as we walked down the sidewalk.

"But then you'd have it for your whole life," said Scott.

"So?"

"It might be something your husband will object to," I said.

"What husband?" Emily asked. "I'll never get married. I'm too big and gawky."

"They'll catch up," I said. "Then the world will see your true beauty."

Emily smiled a little. "Thanks, Kate."

"Hey," said Scott. "I never finished my joke."

"That's right," I said.

"So where was I?" he asked.

"The genie came out of the lamp and gave them three wishes," I said.

"Right," said Scott. "So Moe goes first and he wishes he was the richest man in the world. Next thing he knows, *poof!* it's true."

"How did he know?" Emily asked.

"How did he know what?" Scott asked.

"How did he know he was the richest man in the world?" Emily asked. "Did all his money just suddenly appear in front of him?"

"I don't know," Scott said. "He just was, okay?"

Emily gave me a look.

"It's just a joke," I reminded her.

Plat-a-plat-a-plat! We could hear the sound of rapid footsteps coming down some steps, followed by the rustle of kids crashing through a hedge. In the dark about fifty feet ahead of us, Lewis Larson burst onto the sidewalk carrying a large pumpkin in his arms. He was followed by two of his skater dude pals also carrying pumpkins. They ran away down the street laughing.

"I guess Lewis is building his great pumpkin pyramid," Emily said.

"Wouldn't it be great if he blew himself up along with all the pumpkins?" Scott asked.

"Keep your fingers crossed," I said.

We were just about to start out again when a new group of sounds reached our ears. A bunch of little Power Prince Parakeets were coming up the dark sidewalk behind us. These kids were smaller than the ones who'd come to my house before, and they were talking excitedly.

"Could you believe that place?"

"That howling really freaked me."

"And all that stuff crashing inside. It sounded really real."

"And what was with that candy?"

."Yeah, you'd think that if they had such good sound effects, they'd give away something better than boring lollipops."

"I tried one. They're as bad as the ones my doctor gives me after I get a shot."

Something about that sounded oddly familiar. As the young Power Prince Parakeets passed us, I tapped one on the shoulder.

"Excuse me," I said, "but what house are you talking about?"

"It's a couple of blocks over," the kid said. "Big place with green shutters and white columns on the porch. The sound effects are cool, but the lollipops rot."

The pack of Power Prince Parakeets passed. I turned to Scott and Emily.

"Sound effects?" I said, completely puzzled.

"It must be someone else's house," said Emily.

"Who else has a big Victorian house with green shutters and white columns?" I asked.

Emily and Scott glanced at each other. Neither of them had an answer.

"I think we better go see," I said.

12

About a block away from my house we began to hear faint howling, which grew louder as we got nearer. We turned the corner and started to hear the crashing sounds.

Emily stopped in the dark. "Why are all the lights out?"

That was odd. My house was completely dark. Not a single light was on inside. Only the jack-o'-lantern glowed brightly on the porch.

"Isn't the jack-o'-lantern kind of bright?" Emily asked.

"That's just because all the other lights are off," said Scott.

Aawwwhhhooooooooo! A loud howl came from the house. Goosebumps ran up my arms and legs. "What was *that?*"

"Sounded like a howl," Scott said nervously.

"No kidding," muttered Emily.

"Somebody better go check," said Scott. "Go on, Kate."

"What about you?" I asked.

"Maybe Emily and I should wait here," he said. "Just in case."

"Just in case of what?" I asked.

"Uh, just in case it's nothing," Scott said. "We won't have to waste energy walking back from your house."

"Don't be dumb," I said. "There has to be an explanation for this. It's my house, remember? Inside is the most boring family in the world."

We went across the street and started up the driveway. I couldn't imagine why all the lights were off. Even when my parents went out they usually left a few on. And I knew there couldn't have been a power outage because the lights were on at Mr. Porter's house next door.

Aawwwhhhooooooooo! As we started up the front steps another howl came from the house. Scott froze.

"I think I'll stay here and stand guard," he said.

"Don't be chicken," I said, although inside I felt a little scared, too. I couldn't imagine what had made that sound. I'd never even heard Fred *bark*. But I knew there had to be a logical explanation.

"I'm not chicken," Scott said and pointed at Emily. "She is."

"Am not," said Emily, although she *was* wearing feathers and a beak.

"Listen," I said. "There's nothing to be scared of. This is the world's most boring house, remember? With the world's most boring family. Now come on. Someone's just playing a joke."

We slowly made our way up the steps and across the porch to the front door. A row of windows lined the front of the house on either side of the door. Scott, Emily, and I pressed our faces against the windows and tried to peer inside.

"See anything?" I whispered.

"Nope," whispered Scott.

"Why are you guys whispering?" Emily asked in a normal voice.

"You're right," said Scott.

Aawwwhhhooooooooo! The weird howling came from inside the house again. I felt the hair on the back of my neck stand up, and a shiver ran down my spine.

"Guess we might as well go." Scott quickly started back across the porch toward the steps.

I grabbed his arm. "You're not going anywhere."

"Why not?" he asked.

"Because we have to see what's going on," I said.

"No, *you* have to see what's going on," he corrected me. "It's your house, not mine."

"Just wait a second." I went over to the front door and rang the bell.

Ding-dong!

We waited.

Nothing happened.

"See?" Scott whispered. "No one's home."

"This is very strange. They would have told me if they were going anywhere," I said, pressing the bell again.

Ding-dong!

Again we waited.

Again no one answered.

"Look, it's obvious no one's here," Scott said. "Maybe we should come back later."

Aawwwhhhooooooooo! came the howl.

Crash! Something smashed through one of the windows, shattering the glass.

13

" **A**hhhhhhhh!" Scott and Emily screamed.
All three of us shot off the porch, down the
steps, across the driveway, and out to the street.

"What was *that?*" Scott gasped, breathing
heavily.

We were standing on the sidewalk across the
street from my house.

"Someone threw something through the window." Emily was huffing and puffing.

"Who?" I looked around. There was no one in
sight.

"No, no," Emily said. "I think it came from
inside."

"Inside the house?" I asked in disbelief.

"That's what I thought, too," said Scott.

"That's impossible," I said. "No one in my family would ever throw anything through a win — "

Before I could finish, something round and
white like a Frisbee flew out of the broken win-

dow. It sailed over the front lawn and hit the street.

Crash! It shattered into a hundred pieces.

"You were saying?" Emily arched an eyebrow at me.

"Something very, very weird is going on," I muttered.

"I never would have guessed." Scott was being sarcastic.

I went over to the spot where the thing had crashed, and picked up a small triangular shard. It was hard and white with a blue trim.

"Oh, wow, it's one of Mom's plates!" I gasped. "From her china collection!"

"Duck," said Emily.

"Not a duck," I said. "A plate."

"No, *duck!*" Scott shouted.

Out of the corner of my eye I saw another plate sailing toward us from the house. *Crash!* It smashed on the street a few feet away. This was completely unbelievable!

"Looks like someone is destroying your mom's china collection," said Emily.

"Not to mention the window," added Scott.

I stared at my dark house. This was completely unreal. Mom loved her collection of china, and her house. Suddenly the whole house seemed to glow.

"There!" I gasped. "Did you see it?"

"See what?" Scott asked.

"My house just glowed."

44

"I didn't see it glow," Scott said, turning to Emily. "Did you see it glow?"

Emily shook her head.

"This makes no sense," I said. "I really have to find out what's going on."

"Good idea," said Scott. "Why don't we go to my house and call?"

"No," I said. "We're going inside. Believe me, Scott. There's a logical explanation for this."

"I still think going inside is a bad idea," Scott said nervously. "Don't you agree, Emily?"

Emily looked at me, then at the house. "No, I think Kate's right. We should go in and try to figure out what's happening."

"Traitor," Scott muttered.

It took a couple of minutes to persuade him to come with us. No more plates flew out of the house and the howling had stopped. Slowly and carefully we climbed the steps and crossed the porch. This time I took a key out of my pocket and opened the front door.

Creak! The door squeaked loudly as I slowly pushed on it. That was weird. It had never squeaked before. My father, the engineer, always kept it well-oiled.

I stepped inside. The house was dark and still. Even though I was certain there had to be an explanation for the broken window and plates, my heart was pounding and I was so nervous I could hardly breathe.

45

"Hello?" I called. "Is anyone here?"

No one answered.

"I really think we should go," Scott whispered behind me.

"Wait," I said. "I just want to — "

Aawwwhhhoooooooooo!

At the sound of that howl, I must've jumped five feet in the air. In a flash, Scott, Emily, and I spun around and headed for the door.

But we couldn't leave.

Someone was blocking our path!

14

My legs went stiff. My feet felt like they were stuck in cement. The person standing between us and the door had spiky bleached blond hair with mouse-brown roots. Gold hoops pierced her ears, eyebrows, nose, and lip. She was wearing a black leather jacket with silver chains hanging off it, and tight black leather pants with silver studs. On her feet were black cowboy boots with spurs that glinted in the weak light.

"Mom?" I gasped. "Is that really you?"

I know it seemed impossible, but it looked just like her.

"Hi, sweetheart, what's happening?" she replied.

"That's your mother?" Scott whispered.

"Looks like she's really gotten into the Halloween spirit," whispered Emily.

"Uh, what's going on, Mom?" I asked.

"Things are really hoppin' around here," Mom said. "Come on down to my office, and we'll have some fun." She turned and headed down the hall to her office. When she walked, her spurs jingled.

Emily, Scott, and I shared a wary look.

"Hoppin'?" Scott repeated.

"What *kind* of fun?" asked Emily.

"You got me." I shrugged.

"I thought you said your mom was boring," said Scott.

"She is . . . or *was*," I said. I'd never seen her look or act like that. It was totally bizarre.

"What should we do?" Scott asked.

"Follow her, I guess."

"You sure?" Scott asked.

"No, I'm not sure of anything," I said. "But let's just see."

We started to follow my mother down the hall. *Whomp!* Something crashed upstairs so hard the whole house shook. The chandelier in the hall swayed, and little pieces of plaster and dust fell from the ceiling.

"What was *that?*" Scott gasped, looking up.

"Oh, it's probably just Ben," Mom replied over her shoulder. "You know how boys are."

I couldn't believe her reaction. Normally a crash like that would have sent her racing upstairs in a panic to see what had happened.

We followed Mom through the door of her office and into the waiting room. Usually it was brightly lit and filled with colorful plastic toys and blocks for little kids to play with. But now it was lit by dozens of dripping white candles.

"Wow, Mom, what's going on?" I asked, totally bewildered.

"Oh, we're just trying to get the right *mood*, sweetheart," she replied and went into her examination room. "Come along, dears."

Exchanging more puzzled looks, we stepped in behind her. Like the waiting room, the examination room was lit with dozens of white candles. Mom's back was toward us as she opened some cabinets. On the back of her leather jacket were the words:

MOM WITH ATTITUDE

"Whoever wants to go first, get on the examination table," Mom said. We still couldn't see what she was doing over by the cabinets, but we could hear jingles and jangles as she sorted through her instruments.

"Uh, who wants to go first?" Scott glanced nervously at Emily and me.

"Not me." Emily quickly shook her head.

"You guys are such chickens," I said. "It's my mom. You know she's not gonna do anything bad to us."

But the looks Emily and Scott gave me said they didn't know that. Then Mom turned around. In each hand she held a fistful of scalpels and other sharp-looking instruments. Their blades glinted in the flickering candlelight. When she saw that the examination table was empty, she frowned.

"Oh, come on, kids, who wants to be the first?"

"Fi . . fi . . first for what?" Scott stammered.

"Just a little body piercing." Mom smiled as her gaze settled on Scott. "How about you, sheepherder?"

15

"**B** . . . b . . . body piercing?" Scott stammered and backed away. "Won't that hurt?"

"Just a little," Mom said with a smile. "But isn't that part of the fun?"

I had to smile. "Gee, Mom, this is really great! I can't believe you've done all this just for Halloween. I mean, I think breaking the window and the plates is a little extreme. But it's really good to see you get into the spirit of the occasion."

Knock, knock! Just then, someone knocked on the office door.

"Who is it?" Mom asked.

"Just me," said Doris as she pushed open the door. She was holding a large yellow bowl in her arm and stirring something inside with a wooden spoon. "Just wanted you to know the brownies are almost ready."

"Brownies?" Scott said. "Now *that* sounds good. Come on, guys."

Scott and Emily followed Doris out of the office.

"Guess I'll catch you later, Mom," I said, and caught up to them.

"Boy, if that's your idea of a boring mother, I'd sure hate to see her when she's feeling lively," Scott said as we followed Doris to the kitchen.

"Don't you get it?" I said. "This is a big goof. They're so sick of me complaining about how boring they are that they've decided to do something really exciting."

"Well, they're doing a good job," Scott said.

"*That* is an understatement," muttered Emily.

In the kitchen, baking smells were rising from the oven. Scott and Emily seemed relieved to be back in a normal situation.

Ding! The timer on the oven went off. Doris put down the bowl. Using pot holders, she opened the oven door and took out a tray. "Want some brownies?"

Even though I'd just had dinner, the smell of those brownies gave me a whole new appetite. Doris put the tray on the counter. The stuff inside was brown like brownies, but strange-looking things were sticking out of it — like little wings and claws.

"What kind of brownies are these?" I asked.

"Bat brownies," Doris replied. Then she pointed at something I hadn't noticed before — on the kitchen counter was a big glass jar filled with bats!

16

"*B*at *brownies!?*" Scott gasped, completely grossed out. Most of the bats inside the jar were crawling around on the bottom. A few fluttered in the air near the top, trying to get out.

"Sure." Doris gestured to the bowl she'd been mixing. Inside, half a dozen live bats struggled and clawed through the thick brown ooze. "Isn't that why they call it *batter?*"

Emily and Scott quickly backed away from the counter, but I had to laugh. "Boy, Doris, I can't believe how far you guys are going with this joke!"

Doris frowned. "What joke?"

Thwamp! Before I could promise that I'd never call anyone in my family boring again, something crashed upstairs. The whole house shuddered, and pieces of plaster and dust fell from the kitchen ceiling.

"What was *that?*" Emily asked, looking up.

"I don't care!" Scott gasped. "I just want to get out of here!"

He started to run back down the hall toward the front door.

"Wait, Scott!" I yelled, running after him. "Don't you get it? This is all just a big joke!"

Down the hall, Mom appeared at the front door again, still holding those sharp instruments. "Ready to operate, kids?"

"*Ahhhhhhh!*" Scott skidded to a stop and screamed. Since he was near the door to the basement, he pushed it open. Dad kept his workshop down there. That's where he made things like balusters. Before I could stop him, Scott went down to the basement. I turned to Mom.

"Gosh, I'm sorry about Scott," I said. "For some reason he just doesn't see the joke. It's like he *really* thinks you've flipped."

Mom frowned.

"Anyway, I better go get him," I said. Emily and I stepped through the basement door, but we stopped at the top of the stairs. The basement was even darker than the rest of the house.

"Uh, are you sure this is a good idea?" Emily asked behind me.

"We have to find Scott," I said. For some strange reason I couldn't find the light switch at the top of the basement stairs. I started feeling my way down the steps in the dark.

"Scott?" I called. "I know you're down here."

"Isn't there a light?" Emily asked, following me.

"Couldn't find it," I said.

We reached the bottom of the steps. It was so dark we couldn't see our hands in front of our faces.

Oof! Suddenly I bumped into someone in the dark.

"Scott?" I gasped.

"Shhh! Look over there," he whispered.

At first I didn't know where "over there" was. Then *Zzzzzzssssttttt!* A hissing blue light lit up a corner of the basement. I saw the silhouette of my father wearing a welder's mask as he welded something.

"Come on," I said, slowly stepping toward him.

Zzzzzzzssssttttt! Once again the basement shimmered in blue light.

"Uh, Dad?"

Zzzzzzssssttttt! He kept working and didn't seem to hear me.

"Dad!"

"Huh?" He flipped up the front of the welder's mask and smiled. "Oh, hi, sweetheart."

I could barely see him in the light of the welding torch. "So what's up?" I asked.

"Not much," Dad said. "I'm just working on a new bed for the guest bedroom."

I may have forgotten to mention that Dad was making all the furniture for the house, too.

"We saw Mom," I said. "She's really funny, dressed like a weirdo and looking for bodies to pierce. And Doris is a scream making those brownies with live bats. Is Ben in on the joke, too?"

"What joke?" Dad asked.

I smiled in the dark. "Guess you're in on it, too. So what are you going to do to freak us out?"

"I don't know," said Dad. "Want to try the new bed?" He reached for a switch and flicked on the light.

I stared down at the "bed." It was a large, square board and, every six inches, a sharp, pointed metal spike stuck up through it. Even more remarkable was that Dad was wearing a bright, gaudy, red, yellow, and green Hawaiian shirt.

"What do you think?" Dad asked.

"That's some shirt." I couldn't help smiling.

"No, I meant, about the bed."

"Uh, I think you've made your point," I said with a wink.

"Yeah, I bet that would make quite an *impression*," quipped Scott.

"Lying on it would be a 'hole-y' experience," added Emily.

"Who'd like to jump on first?" Dad asked.

"I'll pass," said Scott.

"Me, too," said Emily.

Dad turned to me. "I guess that means you, Kate. Come on, I'll give you a hand."

"Go on, Dad, give me a break," I said.

Dad scowled. "What kind of break?"

"You know what I mean," I said. "We get the joke. It's really funny. Never in a million years would I have thought you and Mom would do something like this."

"Like what?" Dad still pretended he didn't understand.

"Like *this*," I said, pointing at the bed of spikes. "For the guest bedroom? That's a good one, Dad."

"It is?"

I rolled my eyes. "Okay, okay, so you're going to keep pretending. I guess that means it's time to go back upstairs and see what Ben's up to. By the way, those howls are really amazing. They sound so real. Did you guys finally get a disc player and not tell me about it?"

"I don't have the slightest idea what you're talking about," Dad said.

17

"**A**re you *sure* this is a joke?" Scott asked as we climbed back up the basement stairs.

"Of course it is," I said.

"It is kind of *extreme*," Emily said.

"Well, I guess they really want to get back at me for complaining about them being boring for all those years," I said.

"They've done a good job," Scott said.

Aawwwhhhooooooooo! As we got back into the front hall, that howl met our ears.

"Wow, that sure sounds real," Scott said, looking around nervously.

"Don't be such a chicken," I said.

"I really think it's time to go," he said.

"Fine. Look." I pointed at the front door. Mom wasn't there.

Emily led us through the front door. We went out to the porch and breathed in the cool October night air.

"Feel better?" I asked.

Whack! The sound of an ax smashing into wood made us jump. Wheeling around, we saw Ben standing on the porch wearing a blue wool hat, a red and white plaid shirt, and blue jeans with suspenders.

Whack! As we watched in utter amazement, he swung an ax into one of the porch columns, chopping a huge V in the wood.

"If this is a joke, it's getting better all the time," Emily said.

She was right. After all, there were *limits!* Ben was doing real damage to our house.

"Ben, what are you doing?" I asked.

Whack! "Cuttin' her down," my brother replied.

"Why?"

"That's what outdoorsmen do," he said.

"I don't believe this," I groaned.

Whack! The whole porch shook each time Ben hit the column with the ax.

Scott looked up at the porch ceiling. "Uh, excuse me for mentioning this, but don't those columns hold up the porch roof?"

"That's right," I said.

Whack!

"Then it stands to reason that once he chops down that column, there'll be nothing holding up the roof under it."

"That's probably correct," I said.

Whack!

"And if there's nothing holding it up," Scott continued, "it's likely to fall down."

"Timber!" Ben yelled.

18

We ran down the front steps as fast as our legs would carry us. Out on the sidewalk we turned around just in time to see the white column fall over and crash into the shrubs next to the porch.

Creak! The porch roof creaked and dipped slightly, but it didn't fall down.

Crack! We stood on the dark sidewalk and watched in amazement as Ben smashed the ax into the low white railing that ran around the porch.

"Still think it's a joke?" Scott asked.

"I . . . I don't know," I replied, stunned.

"I'll say one thing for your family," Scott mumbled.

"What?"

"This is a real breakthrough for them!"

"You're not funny," I muttered.

"Oh, I see," said Scott. "I guess you're pretty broken up about it yourself, huh?"

"Stop it, Scott."

"So what should we do?" Emily asked.

Aawwwhhhoooooooo! The howling came from the house.

Whack! Ben slammed the ax into another column.

"Well, I hate to say this, but I'm starting to think everyone in my house has gone bonkers," I said.

"You could say they're cracking up," added Scott.

Crash! Another plate came sailing through another window.

"Hey, guys!" someone yelled.

We turned and saw a large cotton ball lumbering toward us under a streetlight. Bobby-Lee was lugging two overflowing shopping bags filled with candy. He put them down and shook out his hands.

"Man, these bags are heavy," he groaned.

"How's it going?" Scott asked.

"Excellent," Bobby-Lee replied. "I'm about twenty houses ahead of last year. At this rate I'll be finished by nine-thirty."

"Looks like it's time to go home and get some new bags," said Emily.

"Yeah, that's exactly what I'm doing," Bobby-Lee said. "I just thought I'd hit Kate's house and a few others on the way."

"I think you better skip my house," I said.

"Can't," said Bobby-Lee. "This is the year I

trick or treat at every house in Bernardsville. No exceptions."

"But all we're giving are some really junky lollipops," I said.

"Doesn't matter," said Bobby-Lee. "I'm not doing it just for the candy, you know. It's the *idea*. I'm going to be remembered as the kid who trick-or-treated every house in Bernardsville. I'm gonna be a legend."

I stared at him, encased in that huge cotton ball, holding those two overflowing shopping bags of candy. "I don't think you'll have to worry about that, Bobby-Lee."

Crack! Up on the porch, Ben slammed the ax into the second column again.

Bobby turned and looked. "What was that?"

"That's Kate's brother, Ben," Scott explained. "He's chopping down the porch."

"Huh?" The lines in Bobby-Lee's forehead deepened. "Why's he doing that?"

"I guess because it's there," Scott said with a shrug.

Crash! Another plate sailed through yet another window.

Aawwwhhhoooooooooo! came the now familiar howl.

"Gee," said Bobby-Lee.

"Still think it's worth going in there just for a crummy lollipop?" I asked.

Bobby-Lee pursed his lips together tightly. "I told you, Kate. It's the *idea*. If I skip your house then I won't really have trick-or-treated at every house in Bernardsville. I'll just be remembered as a fake."

Crash! This time an old rocking chair smashed through a window on the second floor and landed on the porch roof.

"On the other hand," Bobby-Lee said. "I can always come back later."

19

Bobby-Lee picked up his bags and lumbered away. I turned back to Emily and Scott.

"I think we have to do something," I said.

"As long as it doesn't involve going back inside," said Scott.

"Are you friendly with your neighbors?" asked Emily.

"Yes, especially the Porters."

"I think that might be a good place to start."

"Good idea," I said. "Let's go."

"Wait," said Emily.

"What?" I asked.

"I really don't think we should all leave," she said. "I mean, what if some little kids come along and go in there? Your mom might pierce them. Or your dad might make them lie down on his bed of spikes."

"Oh, stop it," I said. "They'd *never* do that."

Whack! The sound of Ben's ax rumbled through

65

the air as he chopped through the second porch column.

"On the other hand, we'd better play it safe," I said. "Scott, would you stay here and warn people not to go in the house while Emily and I go over to the Porters'?"

Scott glanced back at the house and shook his head. "No way. I'm not staying here alone."

"Nothing bad is going to happen as long as you're outside," I said.

The words had hardly left my mouth when another plate sailed out of a broken window. It was headed right for Scott's head! At the last second, he dove to the ground.

"But you might want to stand a little farther away," added Emily.

"I've got a better idea." Scott got back up to his feet. "Why don't *you* stand here and warn kids not to go in while I go with Kate?"

"Okay," said Emily.

"You sure?" I asked. Frankly, I wasn't sure I would have wanted to be left alone at that moment.

"Just come back soon," Emily said.

"Don't worry," I said. "We will."

Scott and I started toward the Porters'. Their house was next to ours, but their front door was around the corner.

"So what do you think's going on?" Scott asked as we jogged down the sidewalk.

"I don't have a clue," I said.

"It kind of looks like they're destroying your house," he said.

"So I noticed."

"You might even say they're taking a *crash* course in demolition."

"Very funny, Scott," I groaned.

We went up the Porters' walk and rang the bell. A moment later Mr. Porter answered the door. He's a short, round man with a ruddy face and short blond hair.

"So, Kate," he said when he recognized me. "Let me guess . . . Pinocchio!"

"Right, Mr. Porter, but that's not why — "

"Now, let's see if I can guess who your friend is supposed to be," Mr. Porter said.

"It's not really impor — "

"How about giving me a hint," said Mr. Porter. "Is there a theme here?"

"Famous fairy tale liars," Scott said.

Mr. Porter scratched his head.

"Excuse me, but this really isn't the time to — "

"I know!" Mr. Porter stuck his finger in the air. "The Boy Who Cried Wolf!"

"You got it," said Scott.

"Great," I said. "Now I'd really like to tell you — "

"For Pete's sake," said Mr. Porter. "I forgot the candy. Just a minute."

Before I could stop him he turned away from the door and went inside.

"He figured that out pretty fast," Scott said. "Do they usually give good candy?"

"We're not here to get candy," I reminded him. "We're here to get help."

Mr. Porter came back with a big bowl of candy bars.

"Cool!" Scott gasped. "How many can we have?"

"Well, I tell everyone to take one, but since you're a friend of Kate's, you can take two."

"Great! Thanks!" Scott reached into the bowl.

"Mr. Porter, I'm really not here for — "

"Oh, go ahead, Kate," Mr. Porter said. "I promise I won't tell your parents you took two candy bars."

"It's not that," I said. "It's just that they're wrecking the house."

Mr. Porter frowned. "Who's wrecking what house?"

"My parents are wrecking my house."

"Your parents?" Mr. Porter scowled. Then he grinned. "Hey, that's a good one, Pinocchio. You almost had me believing you."

"But it's true!" I gasped.

"She's telling the truth!" insisted Scott.

"Sure thing, Boy Who Cried Wolf," Mr. Porter said with a wink.

"Mr. Porter, please!" I begged. "You *have* to believe me."

"*Your* parents, wrecking *your* house?" Mr. Porter shook his head and smiled. "They've spent the past ten years restoring it. They're the last people who'd do such a thing. But that's a good one, Kate. Or should I say, Pinocchio?"

It seemed that as long as I was wearing my costume, he wouldn't believe me. I grabbed the wooden stick and tried to pull it off my nose. *Ow!* It wouldn't come off!

"Oh, go on, Kate," Mr. Porter said. "You don't have to take your costume off. Just go and have a good time tonight."

The next thing I knew, he closed the door. I would have tried to stop him, but I was still in shock about my nose. The wooden stick really wouldn't come off!

20

Scott and I went back to the sidewalk. We stood there under the streetlight. I was still in shock about my nose. No matter how hard I tried, it wouldn't come off.

"Guess that didn't work too well," Scott said. He unwrapped a candy bar and took a bite. "But at least we got some good candy."

"Scott, I need you to do me a huge favor," I said.

"What now?"

"Take off your clothes."

"Huh?" Scott stopped chewing and stared at me like I'd lost my mind. "Why?"

"Because I want to see something."

"Whoa!" Scott backed away. "Are you feeling okay?"

"I can't get my stick nose off," I said.

"Well . . . I'm glad."

"No, Scott, I mean, I *really* can't get it off. Like it's stuck on."

"Huh?" Scott grabbed my stick nose and pulled.

"Ow!" I yelled. *"That hurt!"*

Scott let go and took hold of my felt hat. But it wouldn't come off either.

"See what I mean?" I said.

Scott grabbed his own hat and tried to pull it off. It stayed firmly on.

"Hey! It feels like it's stuck to my head," he gasped.

"Join the crowd," I groaned.

"What's going on?" Scott asked, his eyes growing wide.

"I wish I knew."

We stood on the corner under the streetlight for a few moments, uncertain what to do next. It seemed like everything had gone crazy, like we were trapped in a spell or something. But why? And how? It just didn't make sense.

"Hey, look!" Scott suddenly pointed. Coming down the street was a police car. The police were always out on Halloween night patrolling the streets to make sure kids like Lewis Larson didn't cause too much trouble.

"Hey, stop!" Scott stepped into the street and waved. The police car stopped and the officer rolled down his window.

"What's up?" the officer asked.

"Uh, she's got a problem." Scott pointed at me.

"What is it, Pinocchio?" the policeman asked with a smile.

"Well, it's my house," I said. "My parents and brother are destroying it."

The policeman frowned. "Who are you?"

"Kate Smith."

"Oh, yeah, your parents live around the corner in the old yellow Victorian," the police officer said. "Your mom's the doctor. They've been fixing that place up for years."

"Well, right now they're doing a pretty good job of unfixing it," said Scott.

The policeman squinted at him. "Who are you supposed to be?"

"Uh, the Boy Who Cried Wolf."

"And you're Pinocchio?" the officer said, looking back at me. "And I'm supposed to believe your parents are destroying your house?"

"It's true," I said.

"Haven't you kids got anything better to do?" the police officer asked. He was no longer smiling. "Why don't you go trick-or-treating like everyone else instead of wasting my time?"

"But — "

Just then the car radio crackled on: *"Officer Ralston?"*

"Yeah?" the police officer picked up his mike.

"We've got another report of a pumpkin theft. This one's over on Flint."

"Ten-four," Officer Ralston said. "I'll check it out." He put the mike back in its holder and turned to us. "Go trick-or-treating, kids. Or go home."

Then he rolled up his window, turned on his flashing blue and red lights, and sped away.

"Well, I guess we better go trick-or-treating," Scott said.

"Why?" I asked.

"You heard him. We either have to go home or go trick-or-treating. There's no way I'm going home."

"As long as we're stuck in these costumes, no one's going to believe us," I said.

"Oh, sure they will," Scott said. "In a couple of days, when you're still wearing a ten-inch stick on your nose, someone's bound to notice. Of course, they may just decide to put you in the nut house."

"And in the meantime, my house will be totally destroyed," I moped.

"Don't forget, you're the one who always wants your family to be less boring," Scott reminded me.

"But I didn't mean like *this*," I said.

"Well, there are worse things in the world," Scott said.

"Like what?"

"Well, Paloma could have assigned us to be Barney and his friends," Scott said.

I stared at him in disbelief. "We better go back and see what's going on. Besides, Emily's waiting for us."

It was pretty obvious we weren't going to get anyone to help us. We went back around the corner to my house. Only, something was wrong.

The sidewalk was empty.

"Emily?" I said, looking around.

"Yo, Emily?" Scott called.

"*Help!*" someone shouted.

"It's Emily!" Scott gasped.

21

He was right. That was Emily's voice. And it had come from inside the house. Except for the glowing jack-o'-lantern, the house was still dark. My brother, Ben, was no longer on the porch chopping down the columns.

"She's in there!" I gasped.

"What should we do?" Scott asked.

"We have to save her," I said.

"You're right!" he said. "We have to save her! We have to do whatever it takes!"

"We have to go in there," I said.

Aawwwhhhoooooooooo! went the howl.

Crash! Another plate sailed through a window and smashed on the street.

Whomp! A television flew out of a second floor window and smashed through the shrubs.

"I have a better idea," said Scott. "Let's keep trying to find help."

"We just did," I said. "No one believed us."

"Well, we really didn't try *that* hard," Scott said. "I mean, we only tried two people."

"*Help!*" Emily cried again. The sound of her voice sent a shiver down my back.

"Listen, Scott," I said. "I'm scared, too, but we can't leave her in there. Something horrible might happen to her. My mom might pierce her."

"Hey, maybe she'll do a good job," Scott said.

"Scott, my mother's a pediatrician," I said. "She's never pierced anyone in her entire life."

"Hey, people have to start sometime," Scott said.

"Well, I'm going back in there," I said. "You don't have to come."

"But then I'll be alone out here," he said.

"That's right."

Scott rubbed his chin and looked around in the dark. "After careful consideration, I think I'll join you."

22

We went up the porch stairs. Every window on the first floor was now broken. Ben had chopped down two of the porch columns, and the porch roof creaked and dipped where the supports used to be. The rail around the porch was smashed and splintered every few feet.

"On second thought, I really think this is a bad idea," Scott whispered behind me.

"Have you got a better one?" I whispered back.

"We could set the house on fire and call the fire department," he said.

"I don't think so," I said.

"What if it was just a small fire?" Scott asked hopefully.

"Sorry." I turned the knob on the front door.

Creak! The door opened and I stepped into the dark house.

Aawwwhhhoooooooooo! came the howl.

"Boy, I wish he'd stop doing that," Scott whispered behind me.

"Who?" I asked.

"Your dog."

"It's not my dog," I whispered. "Fred's never made a sound like that in his life."

"Then who is it?"

Good question. Maybe it *was* Fred. After all, everyone else in the family was acting insane. Why not the dog?

Thwamp! Something up on the second floor crashed. The house shook, and the chandelier in the front hall jingled. Pieces of plaster and dust dropped from the ceiling.

Eeiiinnnnnnnnnn! A loud whining sound suddenly pierced the darkness. It seemed to be coming from upstairs.

"What's that?" I gasped.

"Sounds like a chain saw," Scott whispered.

"We don't have a chain saw," I gasped.

"Timber!" It was Ben.

Crash! Something upstairs crashed to the floor. The house trembled. Scott and I looked up as more plaster fell out of the ceiling.

Eeiiinnnnnnnnnn! The chain saw started up again, followed by the unmistakable sound of wood being cut.

"I think you've got a chain saw now," Scott said.

"Help!" From somewhere in the house came Emily's cry.

"We have to find her," I said.

"Why don't you go and I'll wait here?" Scott asked.

"Please come," I begged.

"But I'm really bad in these situations," Scott said. "I don't handle weird stuff well."

"Scott, *please!*"

"Oh, okay. But I'm not making any promises. The first sign of anything really life threatening, and I'm out of here."

I decided to try Mom's office first. We went down the hall and I stuck my head into the office. The waiting room was still aglow with candles.

"Emily?"

No one answered.

"She's not here," Scott whispered behind me. "Why don't we go outside?"

"Because she might be in the examination room," I said. "Mom could be piercing her right now."

"Well, then you *definitely* wouldn't want to go in," Scott whispered in a trembling voice. "The worst thing you can do is disturb a doctor in the middle of surgery."

I glared at him.

"Then again, it probably wouldn't matter if she were performing an amputation," Scott added with a shrug.

We stepped through the candlelit waiting room. The examination room door was closed and I pressed my ear against it.

"Hear anything?" Scott whispered.

"No."

"Okay, guess no one's there." He started to turn, but I grabbed his arm.

"I have to make sure," I whispered.

"Are you *sure* you have to make sure?"

"Yes." I quietly pushed open the examination room door. Inside, Mom was hunched over the examination table. Her back was to me, but I could see she had a scalpel in one hand and a pronged thing in the other!

"Mom!" I cried. "Stop!"

Mom turned around and looked surprised. In the pronged thing was a piece of meatloaf. On the examination table was a plate heaped with mashed potatoes and peas.

"Here for your piercing, sweetheart?" she asked. "You're early, but hop up."

She picked up the plate and patted the examination table.

"Why don't you finish dinner and I'll come back later," I said and quickly pulled the door closed.

"Emily's not in there," I told Scott. "We better try Dad's workshop next."

I found the basement door and started down the dark steps. Once again it was pitch-black in the basement.

"Uh, Dad?" I said.

"Who's that?" my father's voice came through the darkness.

"It's Kate. Is Emily down here with you?"

Without warning, the lights flashed on. I was almost blinded by the sudden brightness. As my eyes began to adjust, I saw my father standing next to a tall wooden contraption. At the top was a huge silver blade.

It was a guillotine!

Dad pulled the string.

Whomp! The blade shot downward and sliced through something.

Suddenly I saw red!

23

"*Ahhhhhhh!*" A scream tore out of my throat.
"What's the problem, dear?" my father asked.

"You killed her!" I cried.

"Her?" Dad scowled. "I didn't know it was a her. Are there truly male and female watermelons?"

"Watermelons?" Scott repeated behind me.

Dad picked up something green and held it out toward us. "Want some?"

I felt light-headed with relief. He'd used the guillotine to chop a watermelon! The red was the inside of the watermelon!

"*Help!*" A distant voice cried.

"It's Emily!" Scott cried. "She must be upstairs!"

"See you later, Dad." I turned toward the stairs.

"*Someone, help!*" Emily must have been on the second floor.

"Come on!" I cried, heading up the stairs to the first floor.

Scott said, "You sure you want to go up there?"

"Yes, that's where Emily must be," I said.

"It's also where all those howls and crashing noises have been coming from," Scott reminded me.

I stopped halfway up the stairs to the second floor. He was right. But . . .

"I don't care!" I cried. "She needs us!"

"Actually, it might be that she just needs *you*," Scott said, hesitating.

"She needs *both* of us!" I started up the stairs. Scott followed.

"*Help!*" Emily shouted. I looked up the stairs. Emily was on the second floor landing at the top of the stairs . . . *in Ben's canoe!*

Behind her, Ben was climbing into the canoe with a wooden paddle.

"Time to run the rapids!" he shouted and gave the canoe a shove.

Thunk-a-thunk-a-thunk-a-thunk-a . . .

The canoe started banging down the stairs toward us! Ben was in the back, trying to steer with the paddle. Emily was sitting in the middle, screaming, "*Heeeeeelllllllllp!*"

"Run!" I shouted at Scott. We both turned around and started to run down the stairs.

Thunk-a-thunk-a-thunk-a-thunk-a. . . . The canoe was catching up to us!

"Faster!" I shouted.

We took the remaining steps two at a time and jumped over the last four. At the bottom of the stairs was a big long closet where we kept our coats, hats, and boots. Scott and I got to the bottom and dove out of the way.

Thunk - a - thunk - a - thunk - a - thunk - a . . . CRASH!

The canoe slammed down the steps and smashed through the closet wall, leaving a big hole. Chunks of plaster flew in every direction and the air was filled with dust.

For a moment, everything went quiet.

"Where are they?" Scott asked, rising to his knees.

"In the closet, I think." I got up and pulled open the closet door. Emily staggered out. She was still dressed as Chicken Little. But now she was wearing a tan raincoat and one of my father's dark gray fedoras.

"Chicken Little goes undercover," Scott quipped.

"Are you okay?" I asked. "What happened?"

Emily gave me a weary look. "You wouldn't believe it."

"Actually, I probably would," I said.

"Have you been upstairs?" she asked.

"No, why?"

"Your brother cleared it."

"Cleaned it?"

"No, *cleared* it."

"What do you mean, he *cleared* it?"

"He thinks he's a great outdoorsman," Emily explained. "Like Paul Bunyan, you know? Paul Bunyan cleared forests with his ax. Your brother cleared the second floor with his chain saw."

"This I have to see." Scott hurried up the stairs past us. Emily and I followed.

"Do you have any idea what's going on?" Emily asked as we climbed.

"You mean, besides the fact that my family has gone completely berserk?" I asked back.

"You haven't tried to take off your costume, have you?" she asked.

"Actually, I have," I said. "It won't come off."

"Join the club," Emily said with a sigh.

"Oh, wow!" Ahead of us Scott reached the top of the stairs and gasped in amazement. A second later I saw why. Ben really had cleared the second floor. The furniture — beds, chairs, desks, dressers — was all gone. The doorways and doors were gone, too! Most of the *walls* were gone! All that remained were huge holes with jagged edges. The floor was covered with chunks of plaster and splintered wood. The second floor was now one large cavernous room.

"Didn't you used to have a room up here?" Scott asked.

He was right. Everything I owned and loved —
all my worldly possessions were gone!

"Where'd it all go?" I asked, wide-eyed.

"Out the window," Emily said.

I went to the closest window and looked out.
The lawn was covered with broken tables, chairs,
beds, and debris from the walls.

"I bet he had fun," Scott said.

Ding-dong! The doorbell rang downstairs.

Creak! We heard the door open.

"Trick or treat!" a bunch of little voices all said
at once.

"Oh, how sweet, do come in." It was my mother.

"Yes, please come in. I'd like to show you something in the basement." That was my father.

"Anybody want some brownies?" Doris called
from the kitchen.

Emily, Scott, and I exchanged horrified looks.
Some kids had gotten past us! Now they were in
my parents' clutches!

Grrrrrrrrrrrrrrrr!

A loud fierce growl came from behind us. We
were too scared to turn around.

Grrrrrrrrrrrrrrrrr!

"Uh, what's that?" Emily gasped with a trembling voice.

"S . . . sounds like a very big, very mean dog,"
whispered Scott.

"Maybe it's Fred." I turned my head slightly

and looked out of the corner of my eye. Crouched behind us was a huge, wolf-like creature.

Grrrrrrrrrrrrrrrrr!

"Nope, it's not Fred," I whispered. I was trembling so hard my teeth were chattering.

"It might be Halloween Fred," Scott hissed.

"Listen, I read somewhere that dogs and wolves can smell fear," Emily said. "We have to act like we're not afraid."

"How?" Scott whispered.

"Let's turn around and face it," Emily whispered.

We slowly turned. The creature looked like half-dog, half-wolf. It had a shaggy gray coat and was wearing a black leather collar with silver spikes. It had long fangs. Foamy saliva dripped from its jowls.

"Now what?" Scott gasped. He was trembling too.

"Say something to show it we're not scared," Emily whispered.

The dog/wolf snarled.

"Like what?" I whispered.

"I don't know. How about, 'Nice doggy'?"

"Are you nuts?" Scott hissed.

Grrrrrrrrrrrrrrrr! The dog/wolf snarled and stepped closer.

"I have a better idea," Scott whispered in a trembling voice.

"What?"

"Run!" Scott turned and flew down the steps. The dog/wolf lurched forward with its teeth bared.

Snap! It missed Scott by a fraction of an inch!

Emily and I raced down the stairs.

I was certain we were about to be eaten alive!

Only a miracle could save us now!

24

We got back down to the first floor and looked back up the stairs.

The dog/wolf was gone!

"What happened to it?" Scott was gasping for breath.

"I don't know." My heart was beating so fast I was afraid it would burst.

Ding-dong! Just then the doorbell rang again. I pulled open the door. A large cotton ball was standing outside.

"Bobby-Lee, what are you doing here?" I asked, still panting.

"I told you I'd be back to trick-or-treat," he said.

"Listen, this is a really bad time," I said.

"This is the last house and then I'll have trick-or-treated in all of Bernardsville," Bobby-Lee said. "Do you really want to stop me from becoming a legend?"

"Of course not," I said. "But we've got no candy anyway."

"Anyone want some nice warm brownies?" Doris called from the kitchen.

"No candy?" Bobby-Lee raised an eyebrow.

"Brownies aren't actually candy," I said.

"Well, they'll do." Bobby-Lee marched past me down the hall toward the kitchen.

"Watch out for the bones," Scott called after him.

"You can't scare me," Bobby-Lee yelled back. "There are no bones in brownies."

"That's what you think!" I yelled.

Ding-dong! went the doorbell.

"Not again," I muttered, pulling open the door. Outside was Mr. Porter.

"Kate, what in the world is going on in here?" he asked, looking around. "Every window in your house is broken. Someone's been destroying your porch and there's furniture and clothes all over the lawn."

"I told you, my family is wrecking the house," I said.

"Why?" Mr. Porter scratched his bald head.

"I wish I knew."

"Have you seen Sara and Johnny?" he asked. Sara and Johnny were his kids. Sara was eight and Johnny was ten.

"No, why?" I asked.

"They stopped here a few moments ago to trick-or-treat," he said. "I haven't seen them since."

Crash! A loud smashing sound came from upstairs. The house rattled. Pieces of plaster and dust fell out of the ceiling.

"Ben must be in the attic," Emily said.

"What's he doing?" asked Mr. Porter.

"Clearing," Emily said.

Aawwwhhhoooooooooo!

Mr. Porter's jaw dropped. "What was *that?*"

"Uh, it's Fred, the dog," I said.

"I've never heard him howl like that," Mr. Porter said.

"Well, it *is* Halloween," said Emily.

"This is a madhouse!" Mr. Porter cried. "Where are my children?"

"You could try Mom's office," I said. "If they're not there, try the basement."

Mr. Porter hurried off toward my mother's office.

Eeiiinnnnnnnnnn! The chain saw started again.

Bonk! Clunk! Balusters from the staircase to the attic started to bounce down the steps.

"I guess Ben's sawing down the upstairs bannister," Emily observed calmly.

I could only shake my head wearily. "This is just the most unbelievably insane thing I've ever seen."

Scott smiled.

"What are you smiling for?" Emily asked.

"Well, you know how Kate's always wishing her family would act crazy?" he said. "I bet right now she wishes they'd act boring, dull, and normal."

I blinked. "That's it!"

"What's it?" Scott asked.

"The jack-o'-lantern!" I cried. "I made that wish, remember?"

Emily and Scott looked at each other. "No."

"Well, I did," I said, reaching for the front door. "Just before we went out trick-or-treating, I lit the jack-o'-lantern and wished that just for once my family would lose control and act totally crazy. And don't you remember what happened?"

"That big flash?" Scott guessed.

"And you thought it was from some kind of flare," I said.

"Well, it was just a guess," Scott said defensively. "It didn't seem like it could have been anything else."

"I'm starting to think it was," I said as I pulled the front door open. "I'm starting to think I accidentally cast some kind of spell on my family."

"You think that's why we can't get our costumes off?" Emily asked.

"Can you think of any other reason?" I asked. "If I'm right, all we have to do is get the jack-o'-lantern and — "

I stepped out onto the porch. The jack-o'-lantern was gone!

25

"What happened to it?" I gasped, looking around.

"Maybe it fell over and rolled down the steps," Scott said.

We searched everywhere, but couldn't find it.

"This is crazy," Emily said. "Jack-o'-lanterns don't just disappear."

It hit us all at the same time.

"Lewis!" we cried.

We started down the porch steps and out the driveway.

Whack! The sound of Ben's ax smashing through wood made us stop and look back at the house. But Ben wasn't on the porch.

"Where is he?" Emily asked.

Whack! The blade of his ax smashed through the outside wall of the third floor.

"Up there!" I pointed.

Eeiiinnnnnnnnnn! Now that he'd made a hole in the outside wall, Ben stuck the chain saw blade through it. We watched in amazement as the tip of the chain saw started to move slowly along the wall, leaving a jagged line behind.

"Oh no!" I gasped. "He's cutting down the third floor!"

A second later we were running toward Cedar Street.

"Lewis said he was going to blow up all the pumpkins," Emily gasped as we ran.

"If he blows them up, my family may stay crazy forever!" I cried. "My brother will cut the whole house down!"

"Or maybe they'll just return to normal," Scott suggested.

"Is there any way to find out?" asked Emily.

"You could probably look it up on the Internet," Scott said. "Too bad I saw your computer go flying out the window before."

"I think we have to assume the worst," I said. "We better get that pumpkin back."

We turned the corner onto Cedar Street and skidded to a stop. Down the street a large crowd of skater dudes was standing around a tall pyramid of pumpkins.

And at the very top of the pyramid . . . was my jack-o'-lantern!

"Hide!" I whispered. We quickly ducked into the shadows behind a hedge and went into a huddle.

"I have a feeling it's not going to be easy to get that pumpkin back," Scott whispered.

"I think he's right," Emily agreed.

"But we *have* to," I said.

"Not necessarily," said Scott. "You could just get used to living with a totally whacked out family."

"That's easy for you to say," I replied.

"Well, true," Scott said. "I mean, it's easier than saying 'Freddy Freekers wears brown sneakers' four times really fast. But on the other hand, it is harder than saying 'Bobby-Lee Boyle eats bat brownies.' "

"That's not what I meant," I said.

"I think Kate's right," said Emily. "We better get that jack-o'-lantern back. I really don't want to be Chicken Little for the rest of my life."

"How?" Scott asked. "There are about twenty of them and three of us."

"We have to create a diversion," I said.

"Whoa," Scott said. "Big word. I'm impressed."

"This isn't funny," I hissed.

"Okay, okay," Scott said. "You mean, like, we have to create a distraction. Something that keeps them occupied while Emily sneaks in and grabs the pumpkin."

"How come I have to do it?" Emily asked.

"Because Kate's going to create the diversion," Scott said.

"And what are *you* going to do?" Emily asked.

"Me?" Scott swallowed nervously. "I'm going to observe so we can learn from our mistakes in case we ever have to create a diversion again."

"You wish," I said. "You're the one who's going to get the pumpkin."

Scott's eyes darted back and forth in fear as he tried to come up with an excuse not to do it. "But I'm not tall enough to reach it. Emily's the only one who can do that."

He was right. I turned to Emily. "Okay, Chicken Little, looks like you're elected. You hide in the dark and wait while Scott and I draw them away. Then grab my pumpkin and head back to my house. We'll all meet on the porch."

"You're assuming there will *still* be a porch when we get back," Scott said.

"If not, we'll meet where the porch used to be," I said.

"Gotcha." Emily sank back into the shadows.

Scott gave me a worried look. "Now what?"

"It's time to do some diverting," I said.

26

Scott and I wandered up to the crowd of skater dudes. Since they were all facing the pumpkin pyramid, they didn't notice us. Lewis Larson and his friend Alex were standing next to the pyramid, facing the skater dudes.

"Have we got all the pumpkins?" Lewis asked.

"Yeah!" the crowd yelled.

"All right," said Lewis. "See what Alex has here?"

Alex held up a small electronic box attached to some wires that disappeared under the pumpkin pyramid.

"That's what we call a detonator," Lewis said. "Like, you push the button and . . . *ka-boom!* Instant pumpkin pudding."

"Cool!" shouted the crowd of skater dudes.

"The thing is," said Lewis. "You don't want to be too close to the pumpkins when they blow. Otherwise you're like gonna get covered with pumpkin mush."

"Gross!" shouted the crowd of skaters.

They started to move away. It seemed to me that this was a good time to create a diversion.

"Hey, Scott!" I yelled loudly.

"Huh?" Scott was caught off guard. Meanwhile, all the skater dudes turned and looked at us.

"How many skater dudes does it take to change a lightbulb?" I asked.

"Gee, uh, I don't know," Scott replied, nervously watching the skater dudes out of the corner of his eye.

"Ten," I said. "One to turn the bulb and nine to say, 'Far out.'"

I thought that would get the skater dudes mad, but they just scowled at us.

"I don't get it," said one.

"It only takes one to say, 'Far out,'" said another.

"Why are they changing a lightbulb anyway?" asked a third.

"Okay, how about this," I said. "What's the difference between a skater dude and a dead mouse?"

"I don't know, what?" Scott said.

"A dead mouse still has a brain," I said.

"So?" One of the skater dudes scratched his head.

"I thought you said the mouse was dead?" said another.

I started to get the feeling it wasn't going to be easy to create a diversion. Then I had an idea.

"Hey, everyone!" I shouted. "I thought I saw a dime lying on the sidewalk over on Walnut Street!"

"It's mine!" yelled one skater dude.

"No, it's mine!" yelled another.

"Whoever finds it, keeps it!" yelled a third.

The skater dudes took off like a stampede. The wheels of their skateboards made a scraping roar on the street as they raced off toward Walnut to find that dime.

Scott gave me an astonished look. It seemed like our diversion was going to work!

Then I made a fatal mistake. As Alex jumped on his skateboard and started to race past me, I waved and said, "See you around, sucker."

Alex skidded to a stop and stared at me. I could almost see the lightbulb go on above his head. That's when he figured out what we were up to. He wheeled around, cupped his hands around his mouth, and shouted, *"STOP!!!!!"*

The skater dudes screeched to a halt.

"There's no dime over on Walnut Street!" Alex shouted. *"It's just a diversion!"*

The skater dudes all started jabbering at once.

"It's a what?"

"Did he say a diversion?"

"What's a diversion?"

"I don't know, but I guess it's less than a dime."

"No, you dummies!" Alex shouted. *"I mean, it's a trick!"*

He pointed back at the pyramid of pumpkins. Just then, Emily leaped out of the shadows and ran toward it.

"*Stop her!*" Lewis screamed.

Alex took off for the detonator, which he'd left near the pumpkin pyramid, but Emily had a head start. She got to the pyramid first and grabbed my jack-o'-lantern from the top. A split second later Alex reached the detonator and pushed the button.

Ka-boom!

27

Smoke filled the air and we were showered with pumpkin mush. Then white flakes began to drift down out of the smoke.

"Snow on Halloween?" Scott held his palm out.

"Pumpkin seeds," I said. Thousands of them were fluttering down out of the sky.

The smoke started to drift away and we could see someone running toward us carrying a jack-o'-lantern in her arms.

"Emily!" I shouted. "You got it!"

"Neither sleet, nor rain, nor pumpkin mush shall keep me from my appointed rounds," Emily cried. Her white feathers had turned orange.

"Get her!" Lewis shouted.

The skater dudes all jumped on their skateboards, but they either slid off, or their wheels got gummed up with pumpkin mush.

"Use your feet, dummies!" Lewis screamed and started to run after us.

Emily, Scott, and I also started to run, but the

skater dudes were faster. Soon they were right on our heels with Lewis Larson in the lead.

"Give it up, Chicken Little!" Lewis shouted. He reached out and grabbed Emily's feather-covered bag.

"Kate, here!" Emily yelled and tossed the jack-o'-lantern to me.

I caught it and kept going, but they soon caught up to me.

"Scott, here!" I yelled, hoping to pass the pumpkin to him.

"No, no!" Scott held his hands up. "Not me. I don't want it!"

The skater dudes were right on my heels. In another second they were going to tackle me and get my jack-o'-lantern. Then I'd never be able to turn my family back into the dull and boring people I knew and loved.

I'd never have my house back!

I'd never get my room back!

It wasn't fair!

I felt a skater dude's hand clap down on my shoulder. In frustration, I yelled, "I wish all you skater dudes would just disappear!"

28

P^{*oof!*} They were gone.

Scott and I stopped running and looked back in total shock. Except for Emily and some scattered pumpkin mush, the street was empty.

"I don't get it," Scott said.

"What happened?" asked Emily. "Where'd they go?"

"Kate wished they'd disappear," Scott said. "And then, *poof!* they were gone."

All three of us stared down at the jack-o'-lantern.

"It *is* magic!" Emily gasped.

"Incredible!" cried Scott. "Whatever you wish for comes true!"

"Right," I said and started back toward my house. "And right now I'm going home to wish for my family, and my house, and my room back."

"Wait!" Scott cried. "Don't you understand what you're dealing with?"

"Yeah," I said. "A family that spent ten years painstakingly restoring their house until I came along and wrecked it in a single night."

"But it's more than that," Scott said. "You can wish for anything. You can have anything you wish for!"

"Well, I know exactly what I want," I said.

"No way!" The next thing I knew, Scott grabbed the pumpkin out of my hands.

"What are you doing?" I cried.

"Wishing," Scott replied. He hugged the jack-o'-lantern and squeezed his eyes shut. "I wish I was . . . Arnold Schwarzenegger!"

Poof!

29

Emily and I stared in disbelief.

Arnold Schwarzenegger stood before us, holding the jack-o'-lantern.

Of course, he was still dressed as the Boy Who Cried Wolf.

But, you think he cared?

"Scott?" I gasped.

"You better believe it, baby." Scott, I mean, Arnold, I mean, Scott, smiled.

Emily and I stared at each other in disbelief.

"You know, he may have something there," Emily said.

"Give it a try, baby." Arnold, I mean, Scott, handed the pumpkin to her.

"Don't tell me you want to be a movie star, too," I said.

"No way," Emily said. "There's only one thing I ever wish for." She closed her eyes and held the pumpkin tight. "I wish . . . I was a junior size four."

Poof!

30

Emily shrank about eight sizes.

The garbage bag covered with orange feathers looked like a tent with her head sticking out.

"Oh, wow!" she cried, staring down at herself. "It's a miracle!"

"Hey, you look good, baby," Arnold, I mean, Scott, said.

"Here!" The newly petite Emily handed the pumpkin to me. "Wish for something, Kate."

Like Emily, there was only one thing I ever wished for. "I wish . . . I wasn't boring."

Poof!

31

I opened my eyes. Emily and Scott/Arnold were both frowning at me.

"What's wrong?" I gasped, worried that the pumpkin had made a mistake and turned me into a slug or something.

"Nothing," they both said.

"But I'm no longer boring, right?" I said. "I mean, that's what I wished for. You got what you wished for. So should I."

"That's right, baby," said Scott/Arnold.

"Then why are you frowning?" I asked.

"Well, er, I don't know how to tell you this, Kate," Emily began.

"What?" I gasped. "What happened?"

"Well, that's just it," she said. "Nothing happened."

"Nothing?" That didn't make sense.

"Do you feel different, baby?" Scott/Arnold asked.

"No. Don't I look different?"

They both shook their heads.

"You mean, it didn't work?" I asked in anguish.

"Maybe it did," Emily said.

"Maybe you just weren't boring to begin with, baby," Scott/Arnold said.

"But I . . . I *felt* boring," I said.

"Maybe you felt that way because you were always surrounded by boringness," Emily said.

"You think?" I asked.

"I never thought you were boring, baby," said Scott/Arnold.

"Neither did I," added Emily.

"But I *look* boring," I said.

"Hey, looks aren't everything, baby," said Scott/Arnold.

"Well, if that's true, why did you wish to be Arnold Schwarzenegger?" I asked.

"Who wouldn't?" Scott/Arnold replied.

It took a moment for it all to sink in.

"I think we better get over to your house and see what's going on," Emily said.

"Okay." We started to walk back toward my house. We were all tired from running. Since the skater dudes were gone, there was no reason to rush.

"You never finished your joke, Scott," the newly junior-size-four Emily said.

"Oh, right," said Scott/Arnold. "So where was I, baby?"

"Moe just became the richest man in the world," I said.

"Right," said Scott/Arnold. "So Larry goes next, and he wishes he was surrounded by beautiful women."

"And *poof!*" I guessed.

"You got it, baby," said Scott/Arnold. "Beautiful women everywhere."

"So now it's Curly's turn," said Emily.

"And Curly says to the genie, 'Gee, I forgot the question. Could you repeat it again?' "

Scott/Arnold grinned at us. Emily and I scowled at each other.

"Oh, I get it!" I said. "When Curly asked the genie to repeat the question, that was his wish!"

"You got it, baby," Scott/Arnold smiled and nodded.

"That's the *whole* joke?" The newly junior-size-four Emily asked.

Scott/Arnold nodded.

Emily sighed. "I don't know, Scott. I think it loses something over time."

Then, from the next block over, we heard a loud crash!

"*Help!*" someone yelled.

Aawwwhhhoooooooooo!

Some things never change.

32

We ran the rest of the way to my house.

Eeiiinnnnnnnnnn! Ben was out on the front porch again, using the chain saw to cut through another one of the porch columns. He'd apparently given up on the third floor.

"*Help!*" someone yelled inside the house.

"Sounds like Mr. Porter!" I yelled, running up the front steps with the jack-o'-lantern in my arms.

Aawwwhhhooooooooo!

Creak! Just as I pushed open the front door, Mr. Porter came running through it.

"Boy, am I glad to see you!" he cried when he saw me. "Your whole family's gone — "

Mr. Porter stopped talking and stared over my right shoulder. I twisted around and saw that Scott/Arnold was standing behind me.

"Are you really Arnold Schwarzenegger?" Mr. Porter gasped in wonder.

"You better believe it, baby," Scott/Arnold replied with a big smile.

"Why are you dressed like the Boy Who Cried Wolf?" Mr. Porter asked him.

"Hey, it's Halloween, baby," Scott/Arnold replied.

"Oh, boy." Mr. Porter started feeling through all his pockets. "Johnny will kill me if I don't get your autograph."

"Did you find them, Mr. Porter?" I asked.

"Find who?" Mr. Porter asked absently as he came up with a pen and a receipt from the hardware store.

"Johnny and Sara."

"Well, not exactly, but I'm sure they're around," Mr. Porter said. "We'll get back to them in a moment. Arnold, could you sign that to Johnny, your number one fan?"

"You got it, baby." Scott/Arnold signed the receipt and handed it back to him.

"Wait a minute," Mr. Porter frowned. "This doesn't say Arnold Schwarzenegger. It says Scott Swackhauser."

"Oops, I forgot, baby." Scott/Arnold took the receipt back and crossed out his name. Then he wrote *Arnold Schwarzenegger.*

"Wow, gee, thanks," Mr. Porter said.

Aawwwhhhooooooooo!

Eeiiinnnnnnnnnnn!

"Timber!" Ben shouted.

Wham! Another porch support column crashed down.

Creak! The entire porch roof sagged. Only one column was left to support it.

Eeiiinnnnnnnnnn! Ben attacked it with the chain saw.

"Help!" A chorus of children's voices rose up from the kitchen.

"We better see what's going on!" gasped the newly junior-size-four Emily.

I left the jack-o'-lantern by the front door and followed Emily into the kitchen. Six kids in Power Prince Parakeet costumes were tied to chairs around the kitchen table. In front of each of them was a paper party plate. On each paper party plate was a bat brownie with a claw or wing sticking out of it. Doris was standing nearby with a large meat cleaver in her hand.

"Go on, kids, enjoy yourselves," she said.

"We better untie them," I said. Emily, Mr. Porter, and I started to untie the Power Prince Parakeets.

"Hey, don't do that," Doris said, brandishing the meat cleaver. "They haven't had their brownies."

"Scott," I said. "Could you take care of Doris?"

"Sure thing." Scott/Arnold sauntered up to Doris. "Hey, baby, know who I am?"

Doris stepped back and squinted at him. "The Boy Who Cried Wolf?"

"No, baby, I'm Arnold. Arnold Schwarzenegger."

Doris scowled at him. "Who?"

By then we had all the kids untied.

"Run!" I shouted. The Power Prince Parakeets took off down the hall toward the front door.

"Why'd you let them go?" Doris put down the meat cleaver and looked dismayed.

"I think they've already had enough sugar today," I said.

"By the way," said Emily. "You haven't seen a large white cotton ball, have you?"

"Oh, yes, he was here," Doris said.

"What happened to him?" I asked.

"He had his brownies and left."

I felt my jaw drop. "You mean, he *ate* them?"

"In fact, he asked for seconds," Doris said.

"*Ahhhhhhhh!*" A chorus of childlike screams came from the front hall.

33

"**H**urry!" Emily cried.

We ran back into the front hall. The pack of Power Prince Parakeets had made it to the front door. But their path was blocked by my mother with her scalpels and tongs.

"It's a very short surgical procedure," Mom was telling them. "Who wants to go first?"

The costumed kids were trembling and shaking.

"Oh, come on," Mom said. "Don't be shy."

"It's not that, Mom," I said, coming up behind them. "I don't think their HMO covers body piercing. Besides, it's past their bedtimes."

"But it's Halloween," Mom said.

"They still have school tomorrow, baby," Scott/ Arnold reminded her.

Mom focused on him and her jaw dropped. "Arnold Schwarzenegger?"

"In the flesh, baby."

That was our break. While Mom was preoccu-

114

pied with Scott/Arnold, I quickly pulled open the front door.

"Out you go, Power Prince Parakeets!" I yelled.

The kids streamed out of the house.

Meanwhile, Mom was still staring at Scott/Arnold. "If you're Arnold Schwarzenegger, why are you dressed like the Boy Who Cried Wolf?"

"Help!" another voice cried out.

"It's Bobby-Lee!" gasped Emily.

"From the basement!" I yelled.

We left my mom and ran down to the basement. This time the lights were on. Bobby-Lee, still dressed like a giant cotton ball, was lying on the guillotine. Dad was holding the rope attached to the blade.

"Now this won't hurt a bit." He started to pull on the rope.

"Stop!" I screamed.

Dad looked up surprised. "Kate, what are you doing here?"

"I have to ask Bobby-Lee a really important question," I said, kneeling down next to the guillotine.

Bobby-Lee looked up at me with wide, fearful eyes.

"Did you really ask for seconds on those brownies?" I asked.

"Yeah, they were great," he said.

"Weren't they kind of crunchy?" asked Emily.

"You mean, the nuts?" Bobby-Lee said.

"Those weren't nuts, Bobby-Lee," I said. "They were bat bones."

"You guys." Bobby-Lee smirked. "Here I am, about to get my head chopped off, and you're still trying to kid me."

I straightened up and turned to my father. "Dad, do you think you could let Bobby-Lee go?"

"Why?" he asked.

"He's really accomplished something amazing tonight," I said. "He's become the first person to ever trick-or-treat every house in Bernardsville on Halloween."

"Really?" Dad's eyebrows rose. "What's he going to do with all the candy?"

Still tied to the guillotine, Bobby-Lee explained how he'd divide it into 52 Ziploc bags and eat one bag a week.

"That's fascinating," my father said.

"Know how much money I'll save in allowance?" Bobby-Lee said. "Nearly two hundred and fifty dollars."

"Before you said it was nearly two hundred dollars," Emily reminded him.

"That was *last* year," said Bobby-Lee. "I got a raise."

"And it would really be a shame if he lost his head before he got to spend it," I said.

"Oh, well, I suppose you're right." Dad started

to untie the ropes holding Bobby-Lee down on the guillotine.

A moment later, with Bobby-Lee freed, we headed back up the basement stairs.

Aawwwhhhooooooooo!

Eeiiinnnnnnnnnn!

We made it back to the first floor and stopped to catch our breath. Suddenly I realized that all kinds of lights were being shined at the house from outside.

"What's going on?" I asked.

Scott/Arnold stuck his head out one of the broken windows. "I hate to say this, baby. But we're surrounded."

34

Quickly looking out the window, I saw that he was right. Our house was surrounded by half a dozen police cars. They were parked on the lawn with their lights shining at us. Policemen with guns drawn were crouching behind car doors. Behind them were dozens of our neighbors and friends, holding pitchforks and rakes.

One of the policemen had a yellow bullhorn.

"You in the house!" he barked. *"Come out with your hands up!"*

"Do you think they mean us?" Mom asked, coming up behind me and looking out the window.

"Yeah, I definitely get the feeling they mean us," I said.

"Why?" Mom asked.

It wouldn't be easy to explain if she couldn't tell from looking around the house. Every window was shattered. Every piece of furniture was smashed. Ben had chopped down the bannister. There were big holes in the ceiling where the plaster had fallen in. The floors were covered with debris.

"This is your last warning!" shouted the police officer with the bullhorn. *"Come out now with your hands up!"*

"I say we fight," said my father, who'd come up from the basement and was holding a hammer.

"Yeah, we'll never let 'em take us alive," yelled Ben, who was still on the porch.

It looked bad. I knew what would happen even if they did take us alive. My whole family would be locked up for being crazy people.

We'd lose our house . . . or at least what was left of it.

It really wasn't fair. My parents and brother didn't deserve this. Even now they didn't have a clue about what was going on.

It wasn't their fault.

It was my fault.

I'd wished that they'd become wild and crazy.

I should have left things the way they were.

To tell you the truth, they were better the old way.

Boring may be boring, but it sure beats insane.

If only I hadn't made that stupid wish.

That's when I noticed the pumpkin sitting by the front door.

It wasn't too late!

I ran over and grabbed it. Emily and Scott/Arnold must've known what I was thinking.

"Don't!" shouted Emily, who was still enjoying being a junior size four.

"Please don't, baby!" yelled Scott/Arnold.

"Sorry, guys." I shut my eyes and hugged the jack-o'-lantern. "I wish everything would go back to normal!"

Smash! I threw the pumpkin to the floor.

"Hasta la vista, baby," Scott/Arnold muttered.

Poof!

35

The next thing I knew, everything went back to normal, *almost*. My mother was dressed in her normal, boring brown clothes again. But she still had the scalpels and other instruments in her hands.

"What am I doing with these?" she asked, bewildered.

Next to her, my father's face turned pale as he looked down at the bright and gaudy Hawaiian shirt. "Why am I wearing *this*?"

"I'm feeling very tired, dear," said my mother. "I think it's time to go to bed."

"I agree," said Dad.

She and Dad started up the stairs. All the damage had disappeared. Halfway up, Mom turned to me. She pointed at the smashed pumpkin on the floor. "Kate, darling, be a dear and clean up that mess, will you?"

Then she and my father went upstairs.

The front door swung open and Ben trudged in, carrying the ax and chain saw.

"I have the weirdest feeling," he groaned. "Like I just destroyed a house. And what am I doing with an ax and a chain saw? I didn't know we even *owned* a chain saw."

Emily, Scott, and I gave each other nervous looks.

Then Ben yawned. "Whew, I'm beat. Think I'll go to bed."

He climbed the stairs.

Through the open front door we could see the policemen standing around their cars with bewildered looks on their faces. The big crowd of neighbors looked puzzled, too, as if they couldn't figure out why they were standing around in the dark holding rakes and pitchforks.

The police officer with the bullhorn turned and aimed it at them.

"*All right, folks, let's break it up,*" he yelled. "*Everyone go home.*"

We watched everyone start to walk away. Then the policemen got in their cars and backed them off the lawn. I was just about to close the front door when I heard a familiar scraping sound. Coming down the street was Lewis Larson, followed by a dozen skater dudes.

"Oh, darn," Emily muttered. "I was hoping it wouldn't *all* go back to the way it used to be."

"I hate to say it, but it's better this way," I said.

"Maybe for *you*," said Scott who was a shrimp again.

"It was pretty neat being a junior size four," added Emily, who was big and gawky again. Then she pulled off her cardboard beak and the plastic bag covered with feathers. "But at least I won't have to wear this stuff for the rest of my life."

The basement door swung open, and Bobby-Lee trudged through it, carrying two bulging shopping bags of candy.

"Think there are any brownies left?" he asked.

"I hate to say it, but they're probably gone," I said.

"Oh, well, then I guess I better go home," Bobby-Lee said. "I've still got a couple of hours of work left dividing up all this stuff."

He went out the door.

"Guess I'll go home, too," said Emily. "One thing's for sure. I'll never forget *this* Halloween."

"You don't mind that I made that wish and turned everything boring again, do you?" I asked.

"Well . . ." Emily sighed wistfully. "It *was* kind of fun, but I guess I'll live. Bye."

She went out. I turned to Scott.

"Yeah, might as well go," he said.

I blocked his path for a second. "Remember

what you said before? About me not being boring? Did you really mean it?"

"Sure," Scott said. "I never thought you were boring. You're funny and talkative and cool to be with."

I couldn't help smiling. "Gee, Scott, thanks."

"Now could you do me a favor?" he said.

"Sure. What?"

"Could you change me back into Arnold again?"

I smiled and shook my head. "Believe me, if I could, I would."

Scott nodded sadly. "I figured. See you tomorrow, Kate."

I watched him leave. Then I locked the door.

Yip! Fred came down the steps, looking like the same old boring mutt. I patted him on the head, then cleaned up the smashed pumpkin on the floor. By then it was late and I was tired. Wow, what a night.

I went upstairs and got into bed. Outside I could hear a few *bangs!* and *pops!* as kids shot off the last of their fireworks. I snuggled under the covers and thought about what Scott had said.

I wasn't boring.

Maybe it really doesn't matter what you look like or what your parents are like.

Maybe it really is what's inside that counts.

I yawned and rubbed my eyes. I was tired and looking forward to a good night's sleep.

I closed my eyes, very glad that everything was back to normal.

Aawwwhhhooooooooo! Suddenly a howl split the silence.

Well . . . *almost* normal.

About the Author

Todd Strasser has written many award-winning novels for young and teenage readers. Among his best known are *Help! I'm Trapped in the First Day of School; Help! I'm Trapped in My Teacher's Body;* and *Please* Don't *Be Mine, Julie Valentine!* His next project for Scholastic will be a series about a dog detective named Furry Mason.

Mr. Strasser speaks frequently at schools about the craft of writing and conducts writing workshops for young people. He lives in a suburb of New York City with his wife, children, and Labrador retriever.